Welcome to the whimsical world of Detective Sparklehoof!

When the town's glitter mysteriously disappears, it's up to Sparklehoof - the cleverest unicorn detective around - to follow the clues, meet curious creatures, and solve the mystery!

As you color each page, you'll travel through donut shops, cloud parks, rivers and cozy forests!

Grab your favourite colors, and help bring the sparkle back to town!

Key Characters

Detective Sparklehooff

Detective Sparklehoof is always ready for an adventure! With her trusty magnifying glass and detective hat, she solves mysteries with kindness, curiosity, and a little bit of sparkle!

Ollie the Wise Owl

Ollie is the forest's wisest creature. He's full of ancient knowledge and always ready to lend a helping wing to Detective Sparklehoof!

Key Characters

Squeaky the Squirrel

Squeaky is a curious and mischievous squirrel who loves shiny things! They are always ready to help, especially when it comes to finding the sparkliest clues!

Flicker the Fairy Baker

Flicker is a tiny, cheerful fairy with a love for baking glittery cupcakes. She brings sweetness to every mystery — and to every case Sparklehoof solves!

Key Characters

Puff the Glitter Dragon

Puff is a friendly dragon who accidentally sneezes glitter! He's always happy to help, even if his glittery hiccups make the case a little messier!

Ready to start your adventure with Detective Sparklehoof?

Let's make sure you have all the essential gear!

CHECK LIST

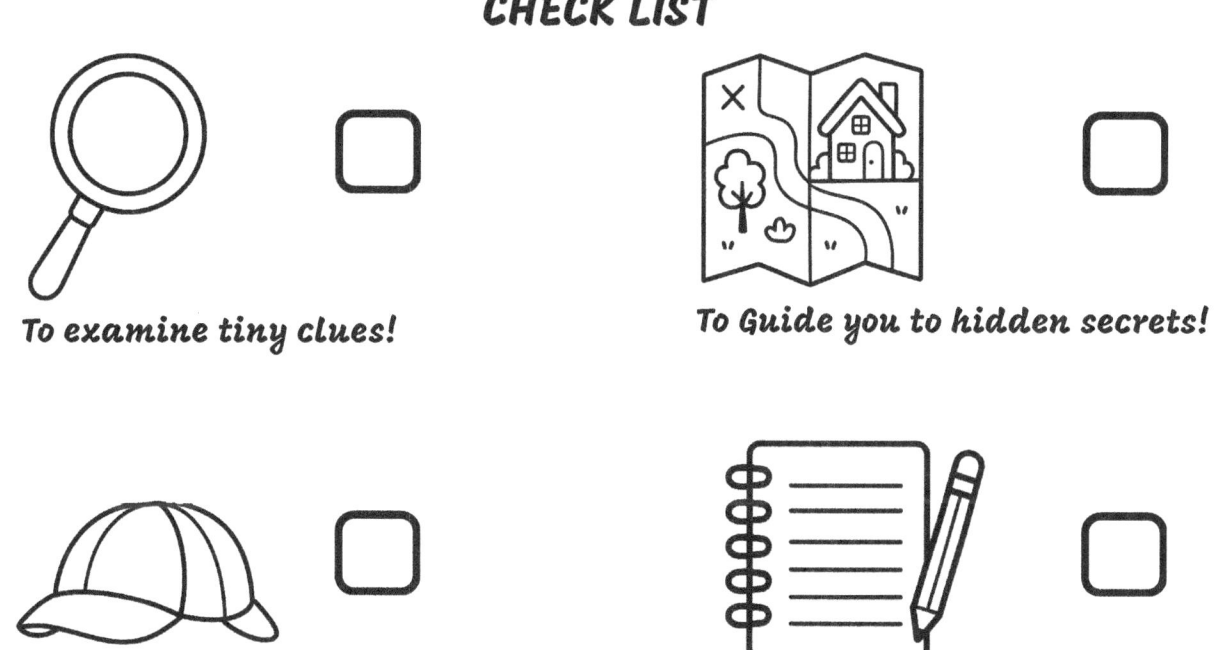

To examine tiny clues!

To Guide you to hidden secrets!

For that official detective look!

For writing down clues that are important

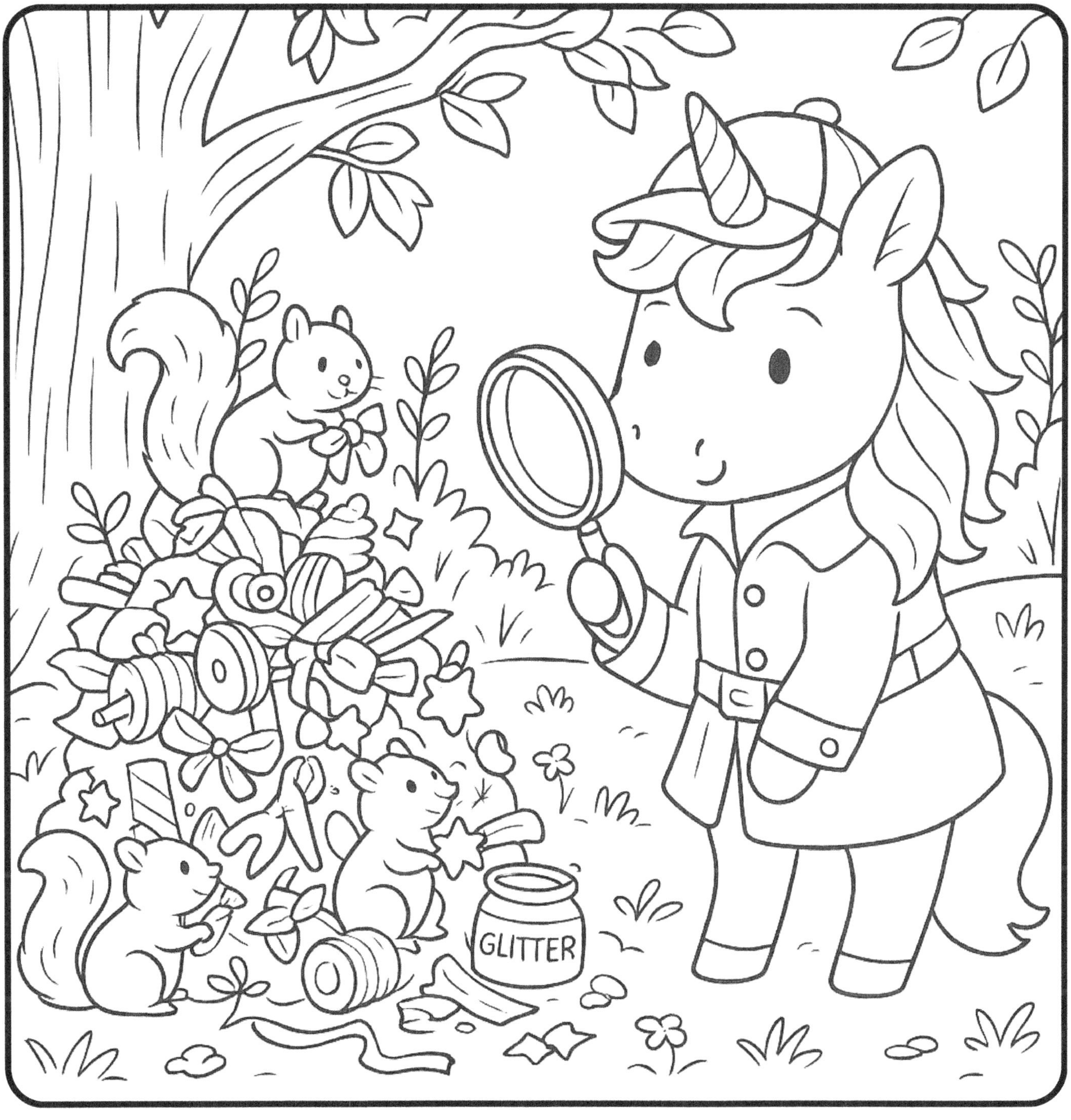
GLITTER

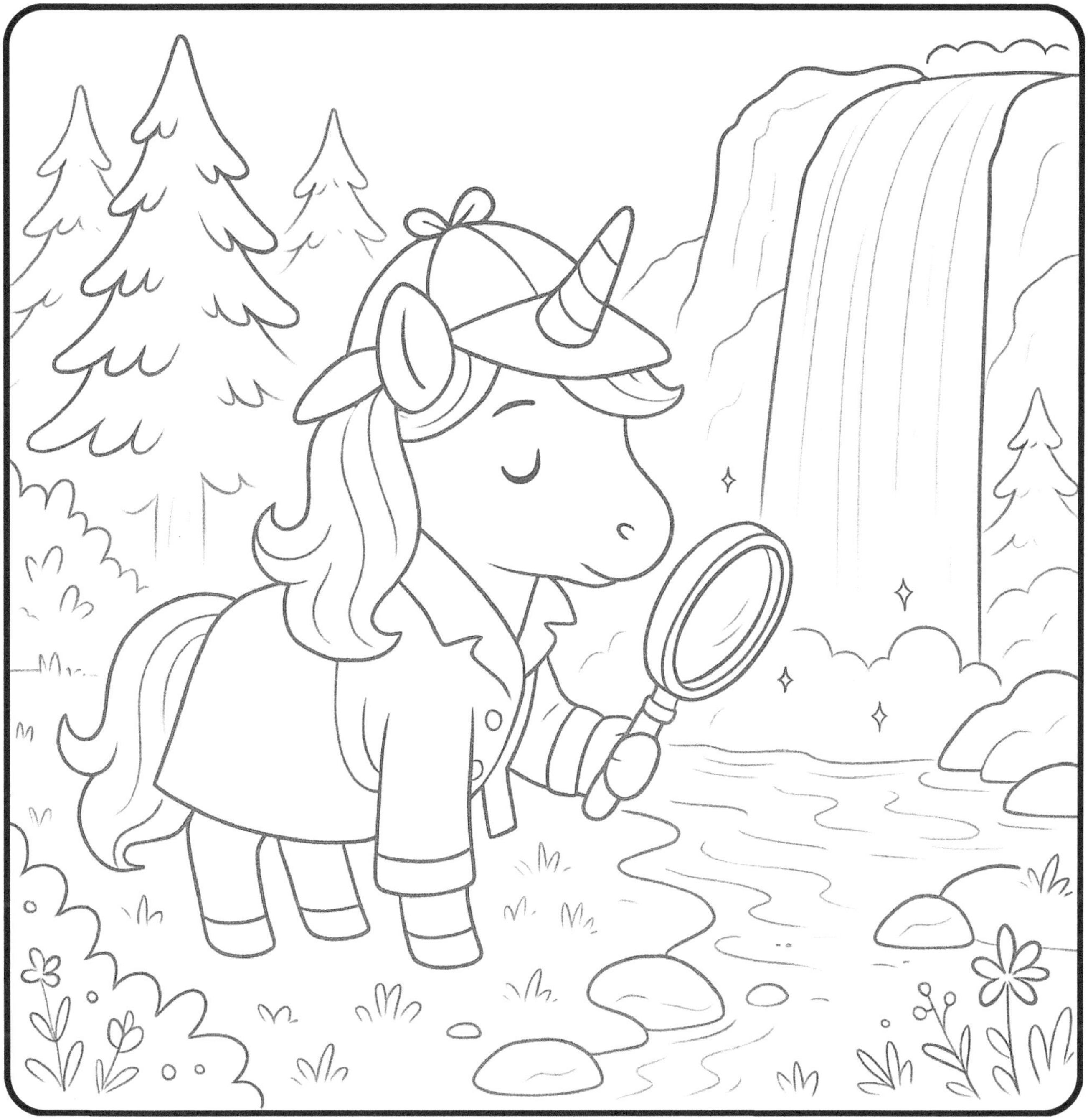

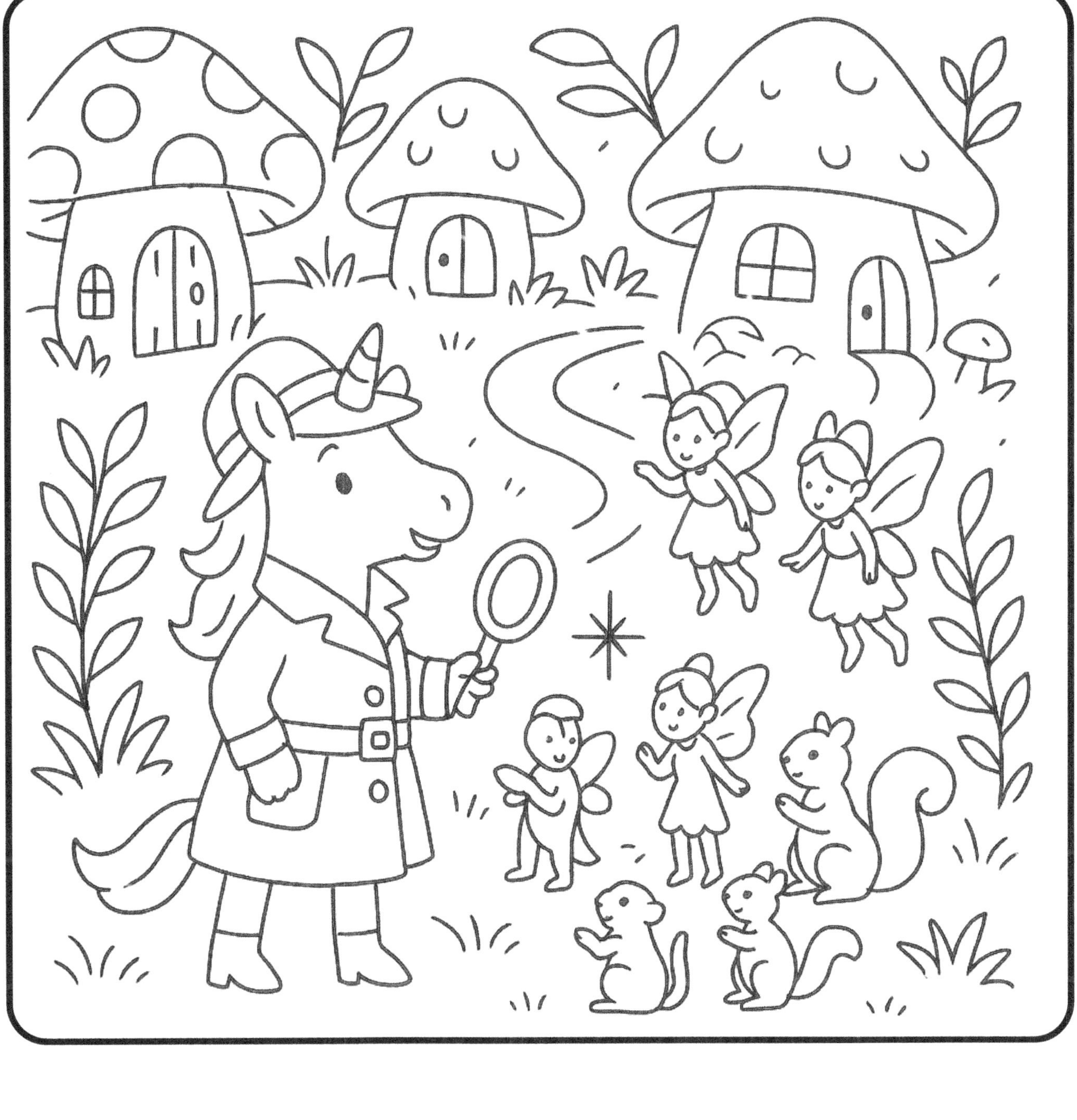

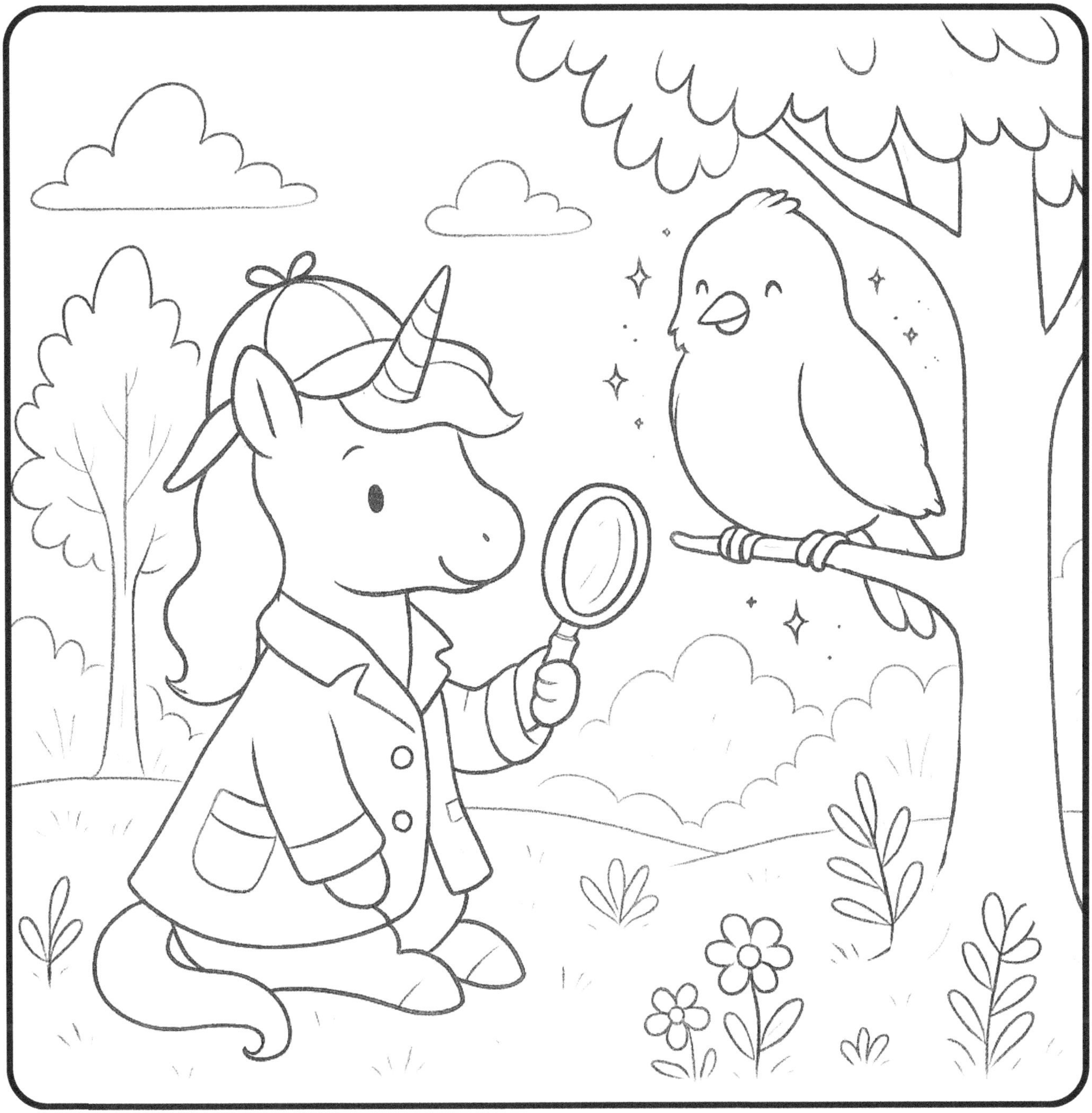

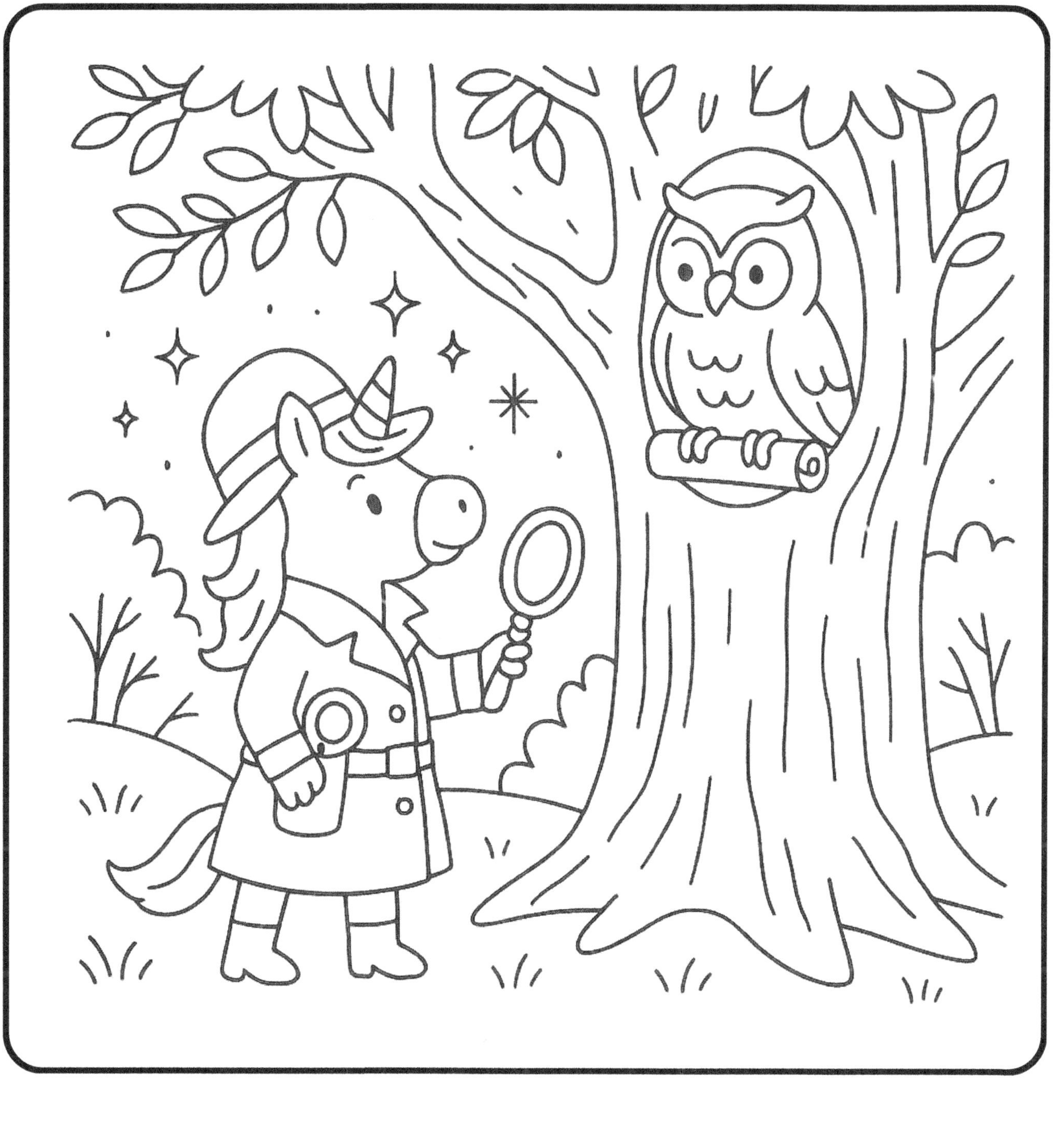

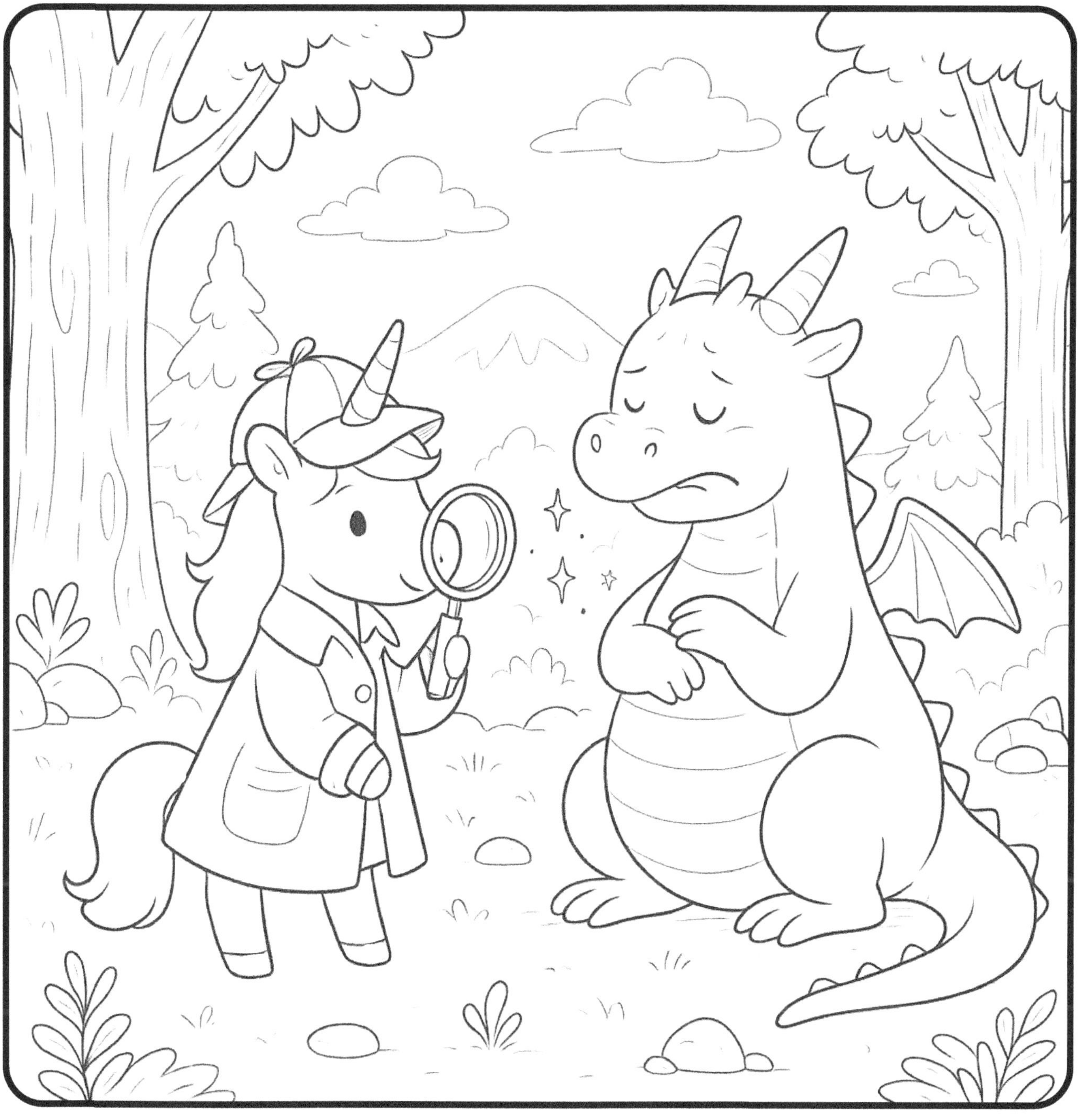

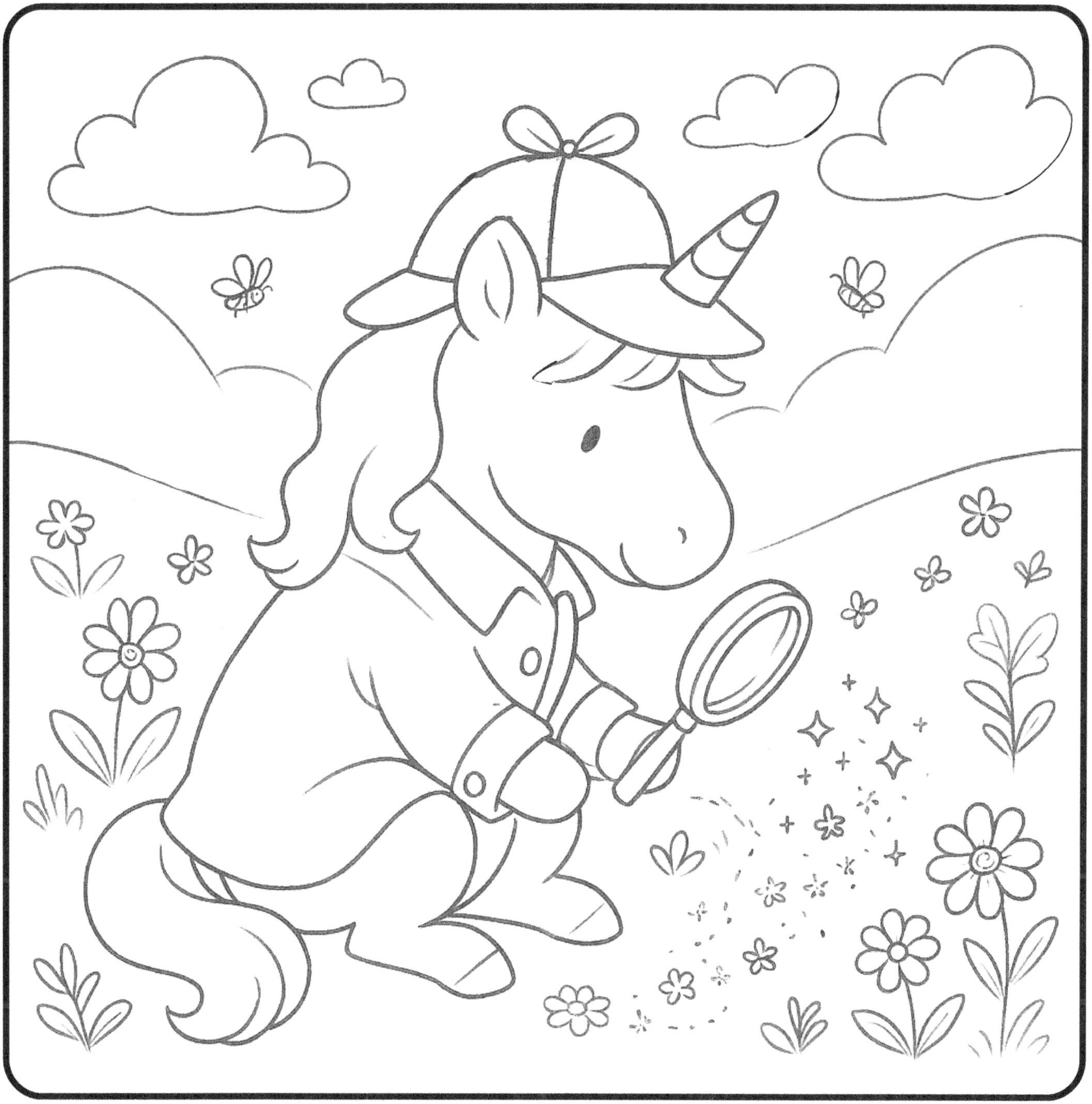

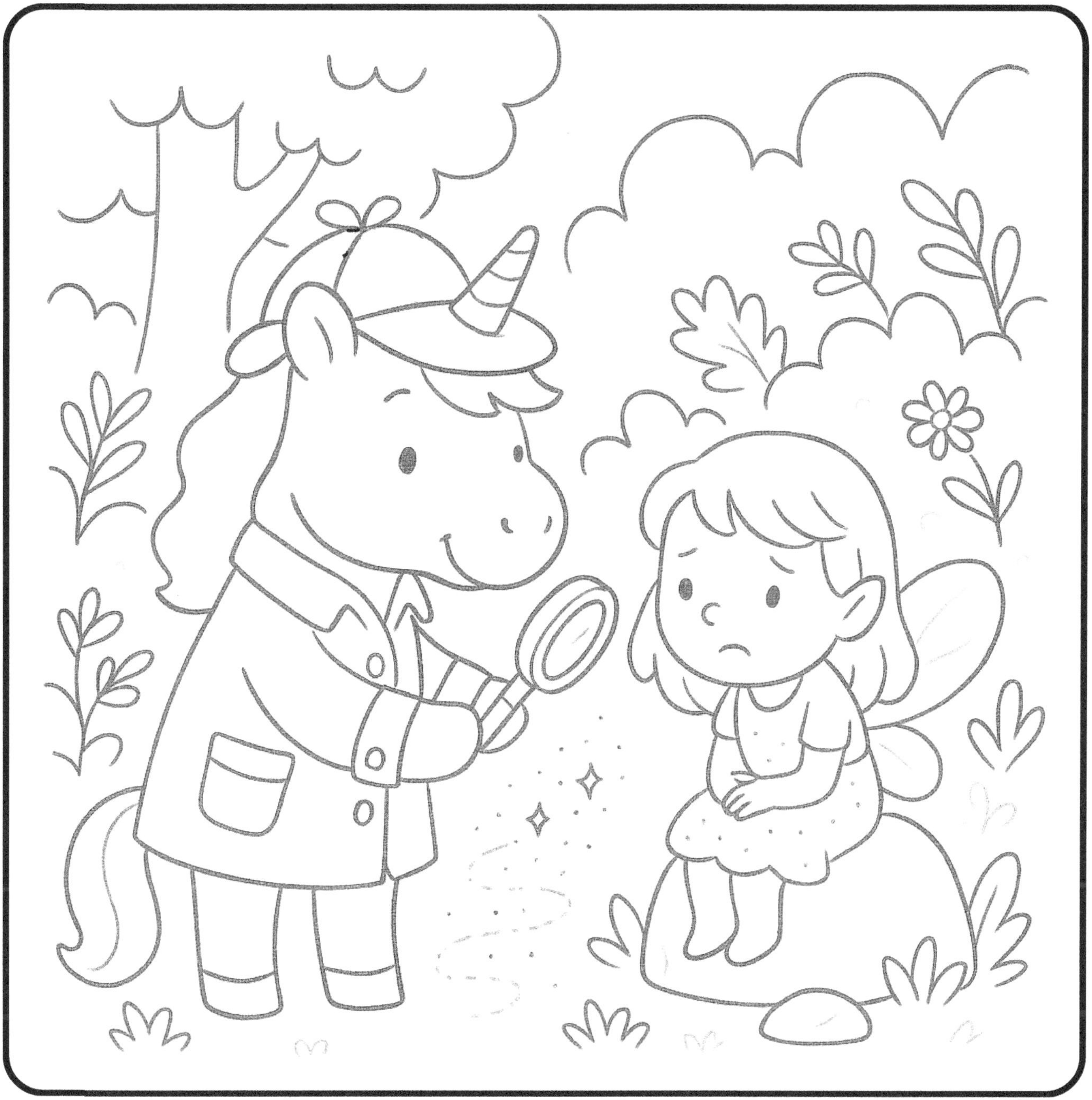

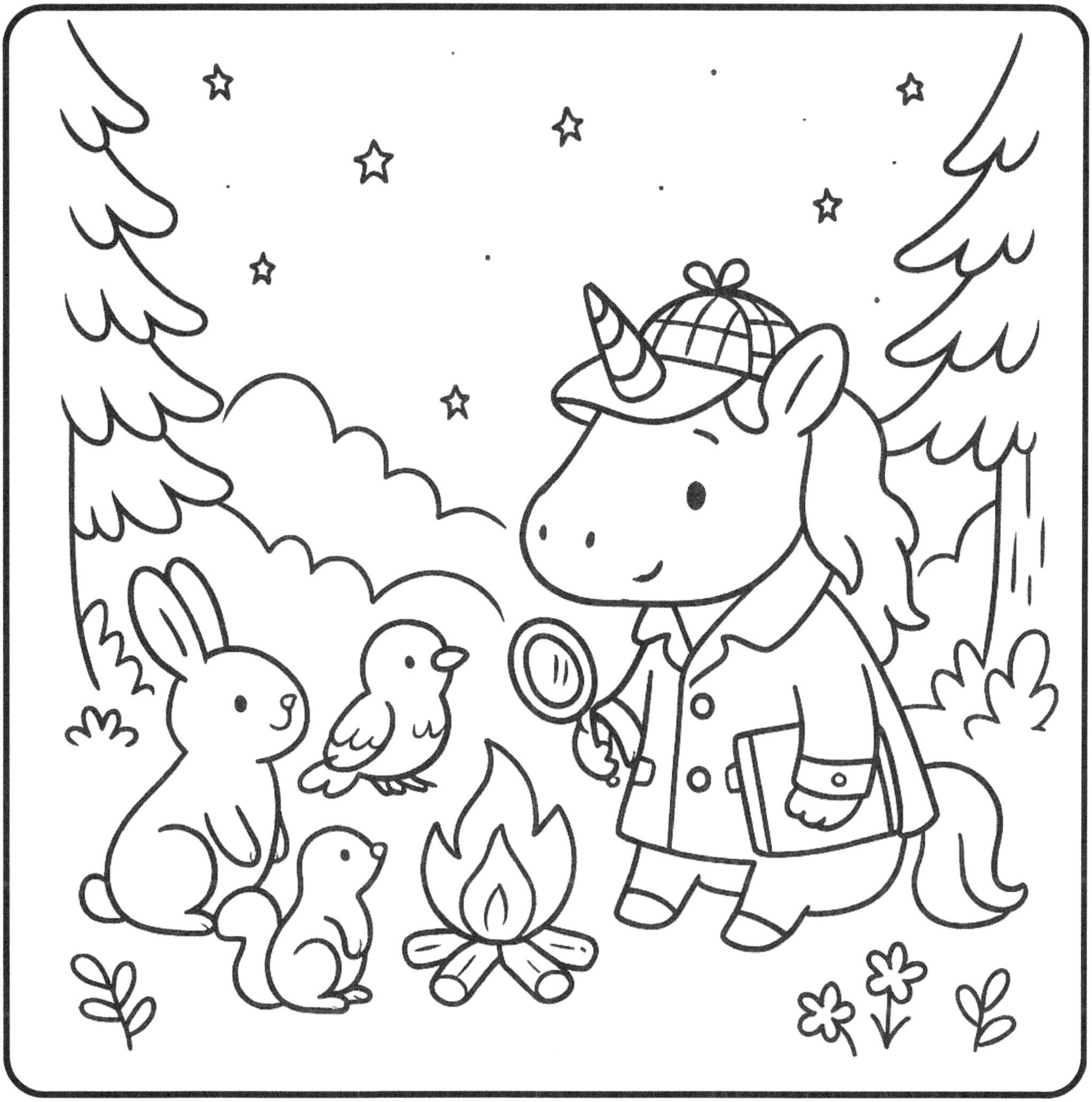

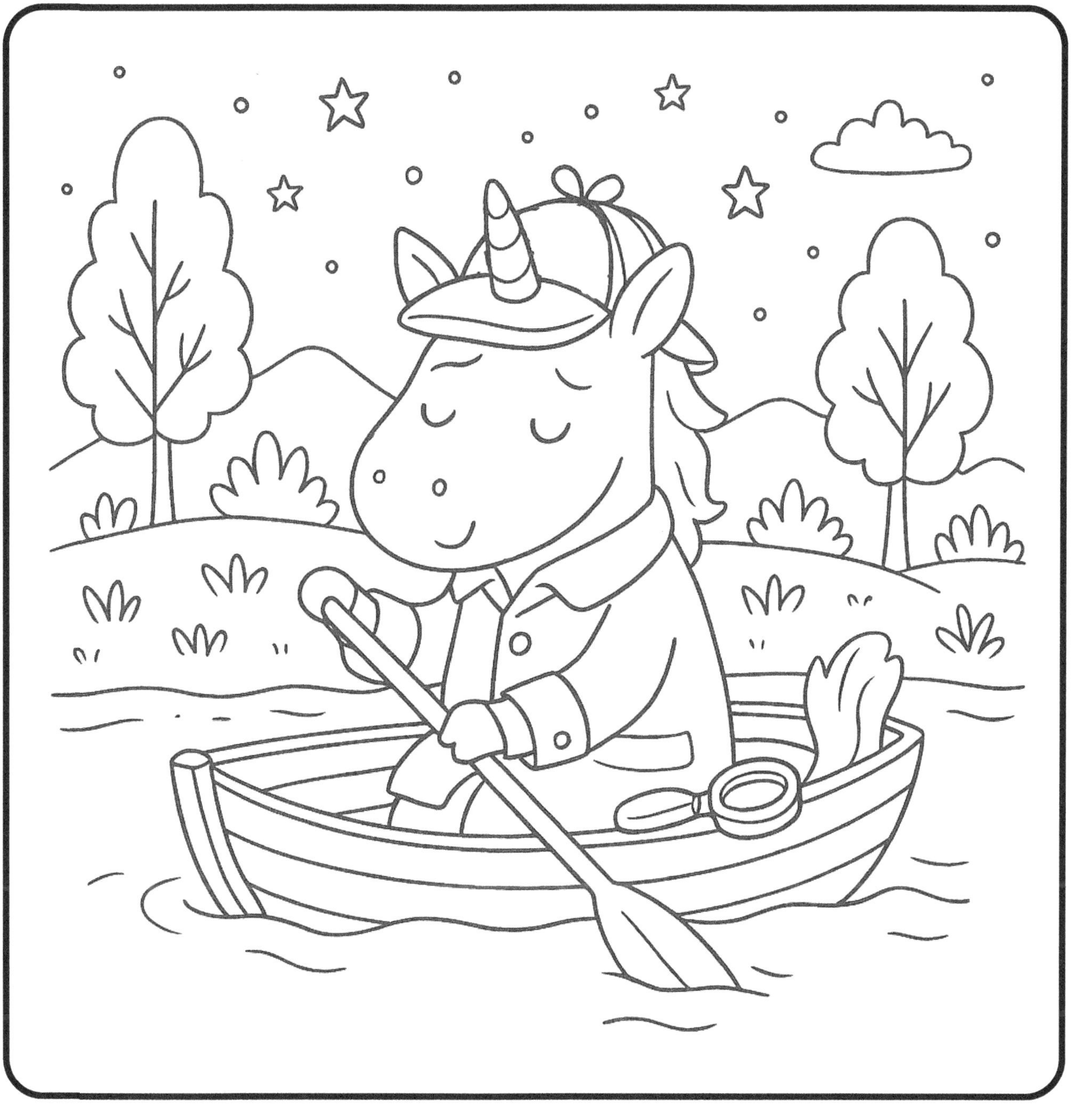

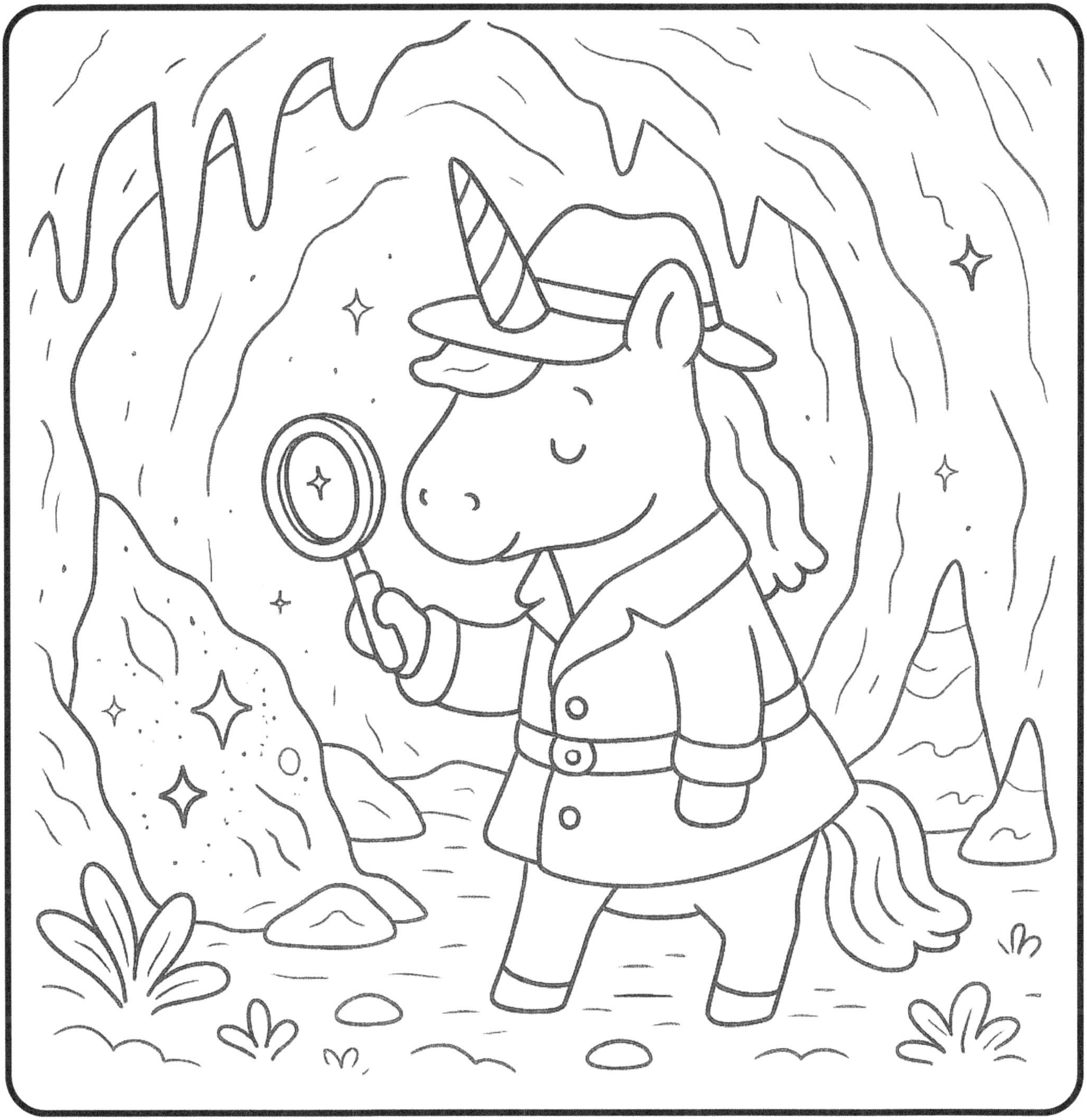

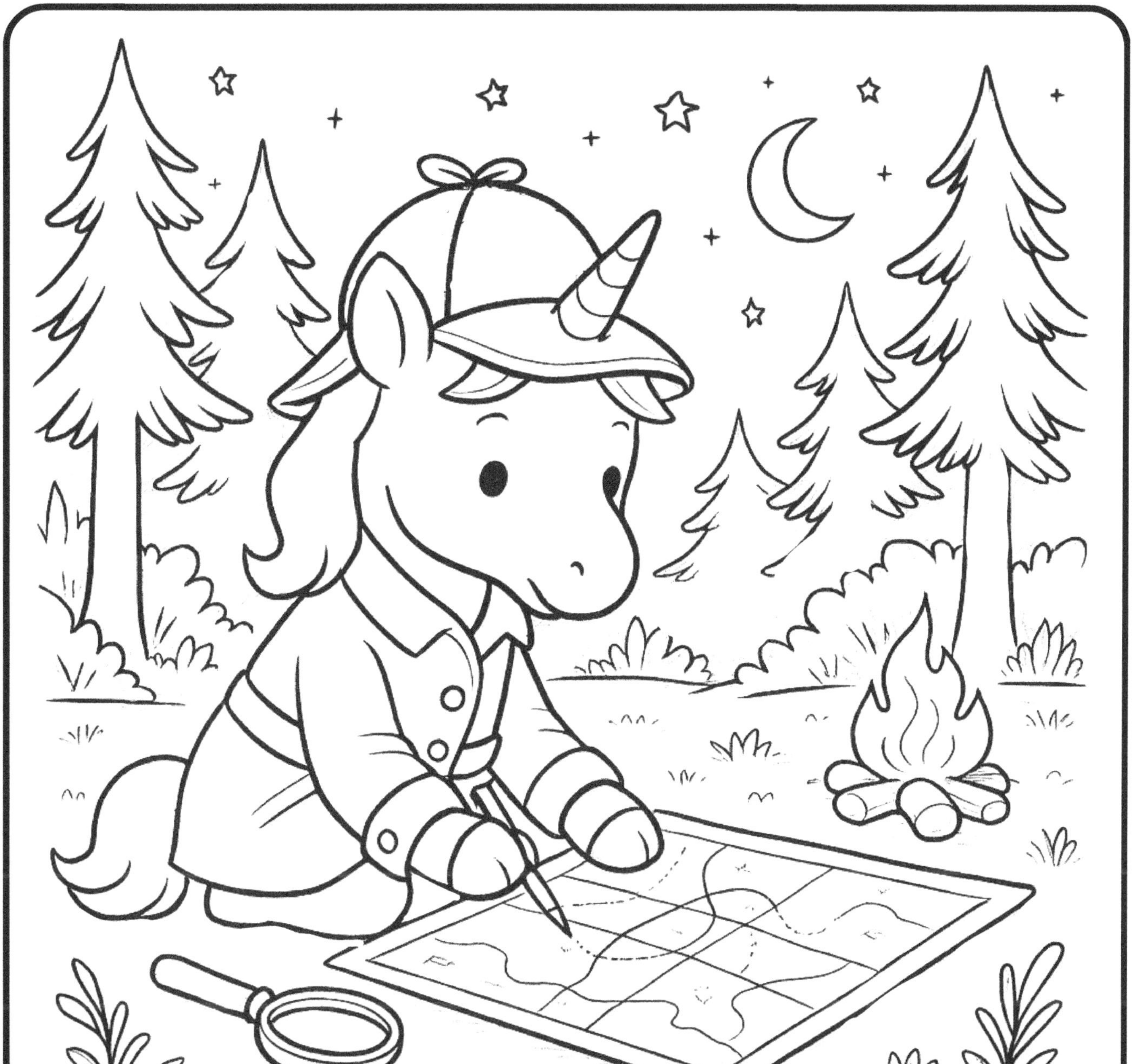

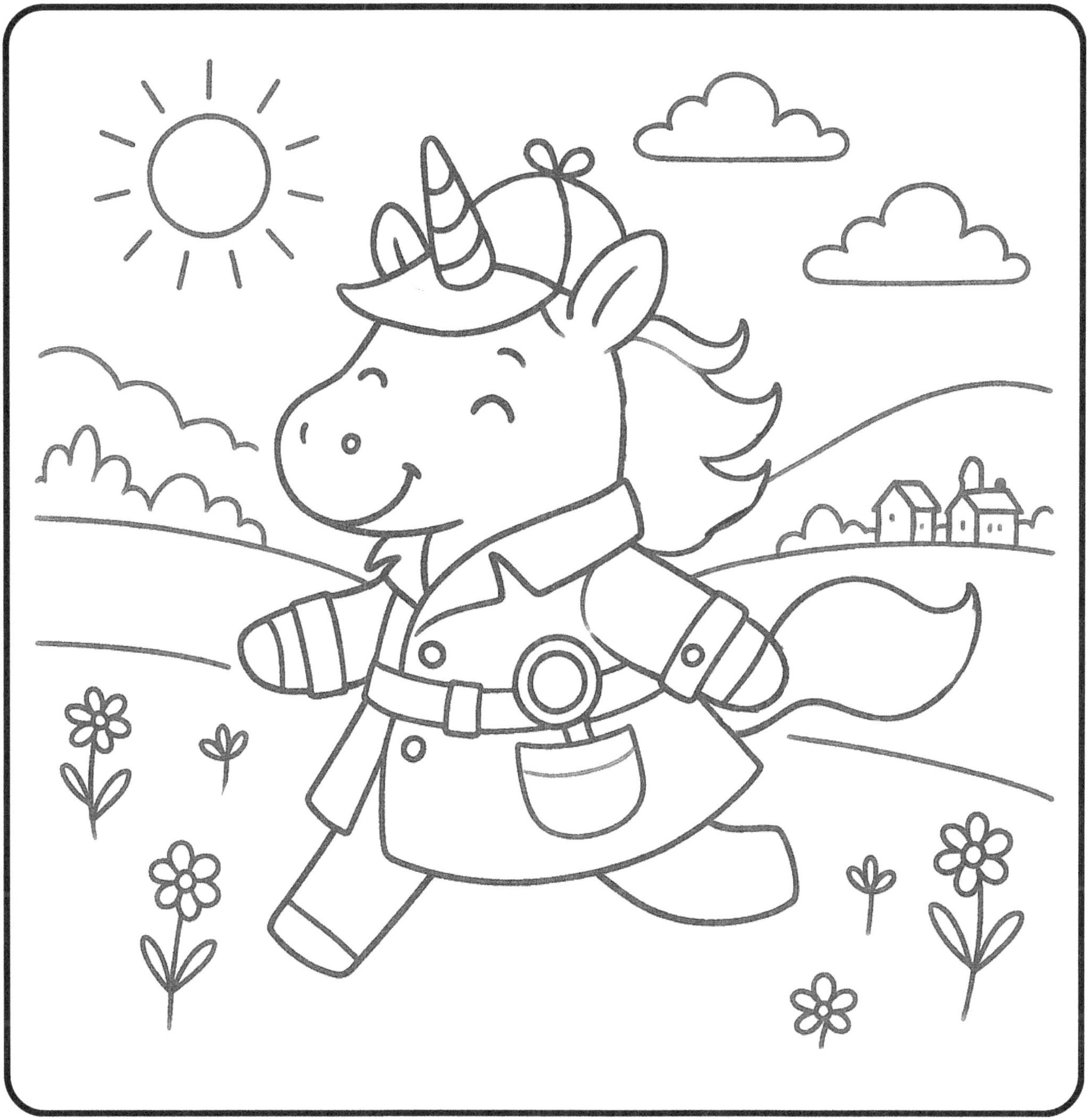

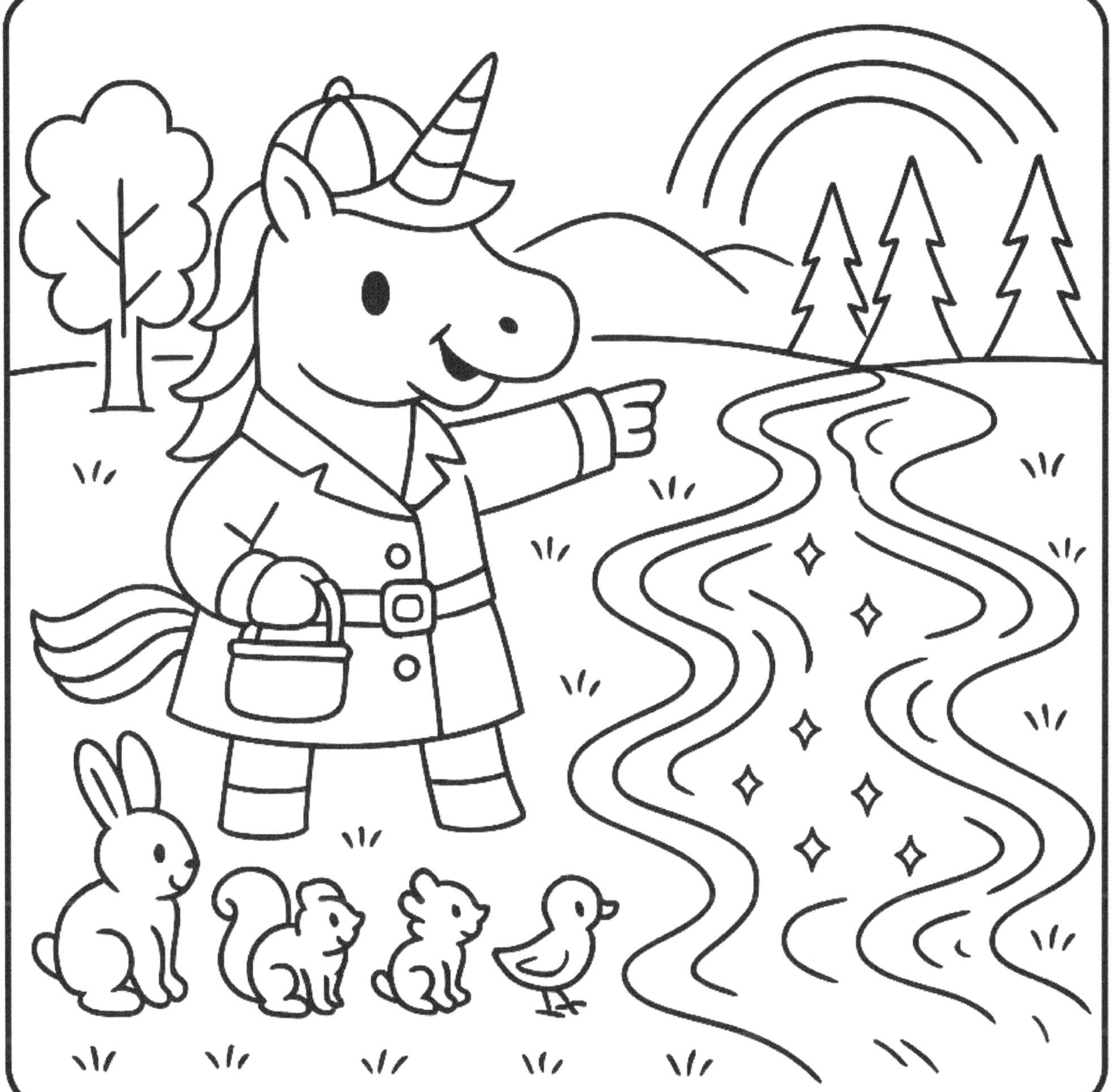

THANK YOU, SPARKLEHOOF!

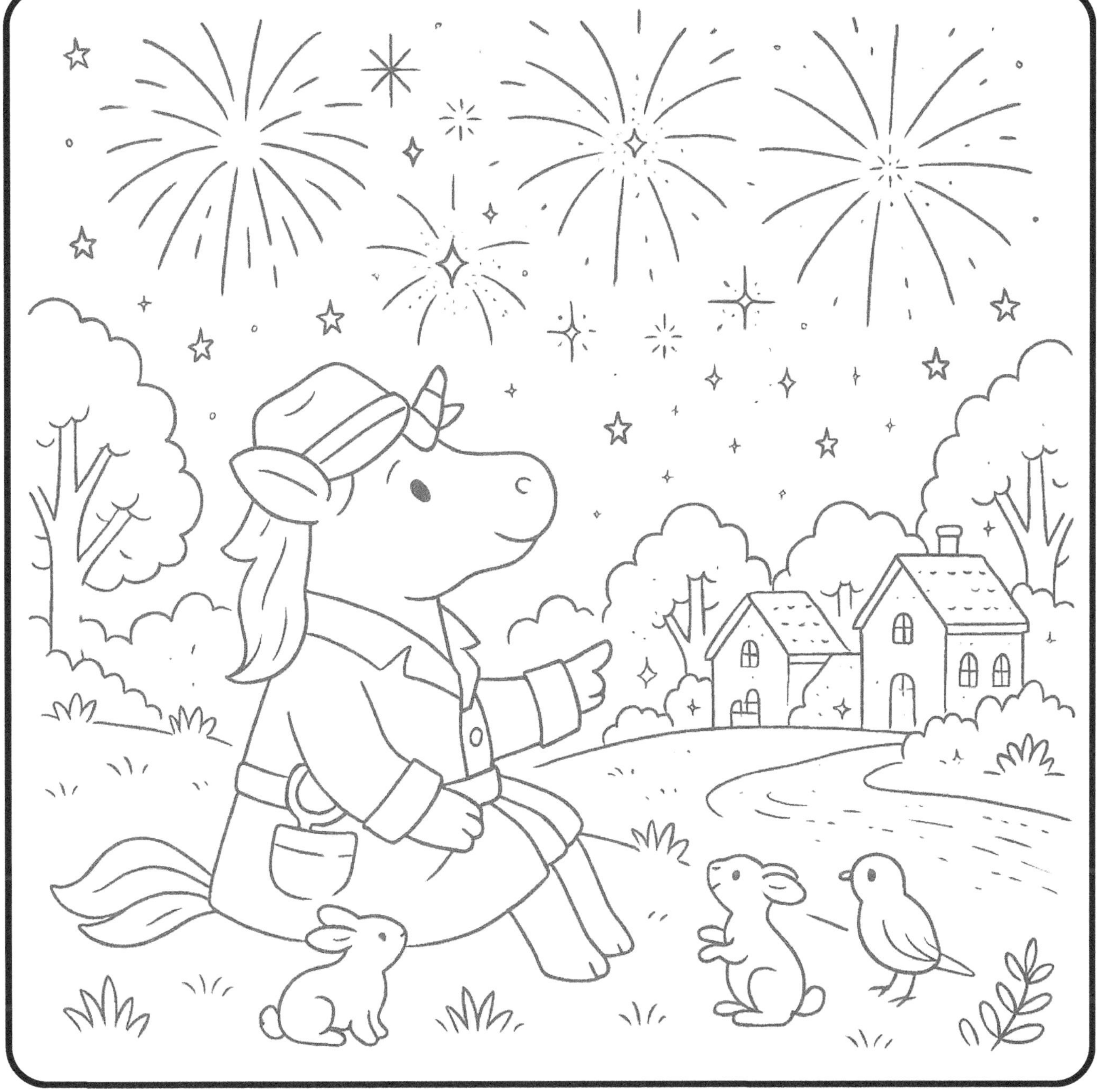

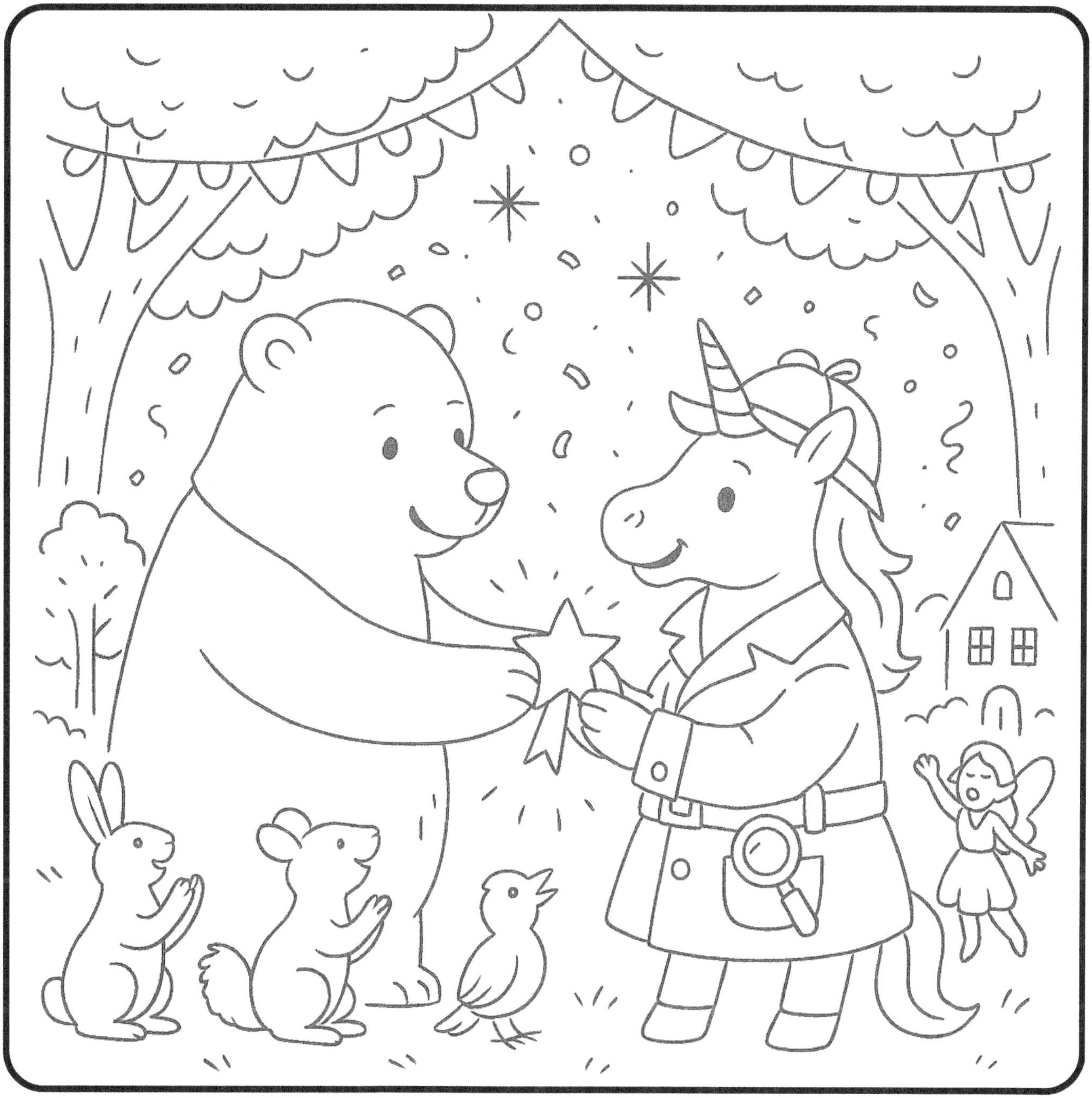

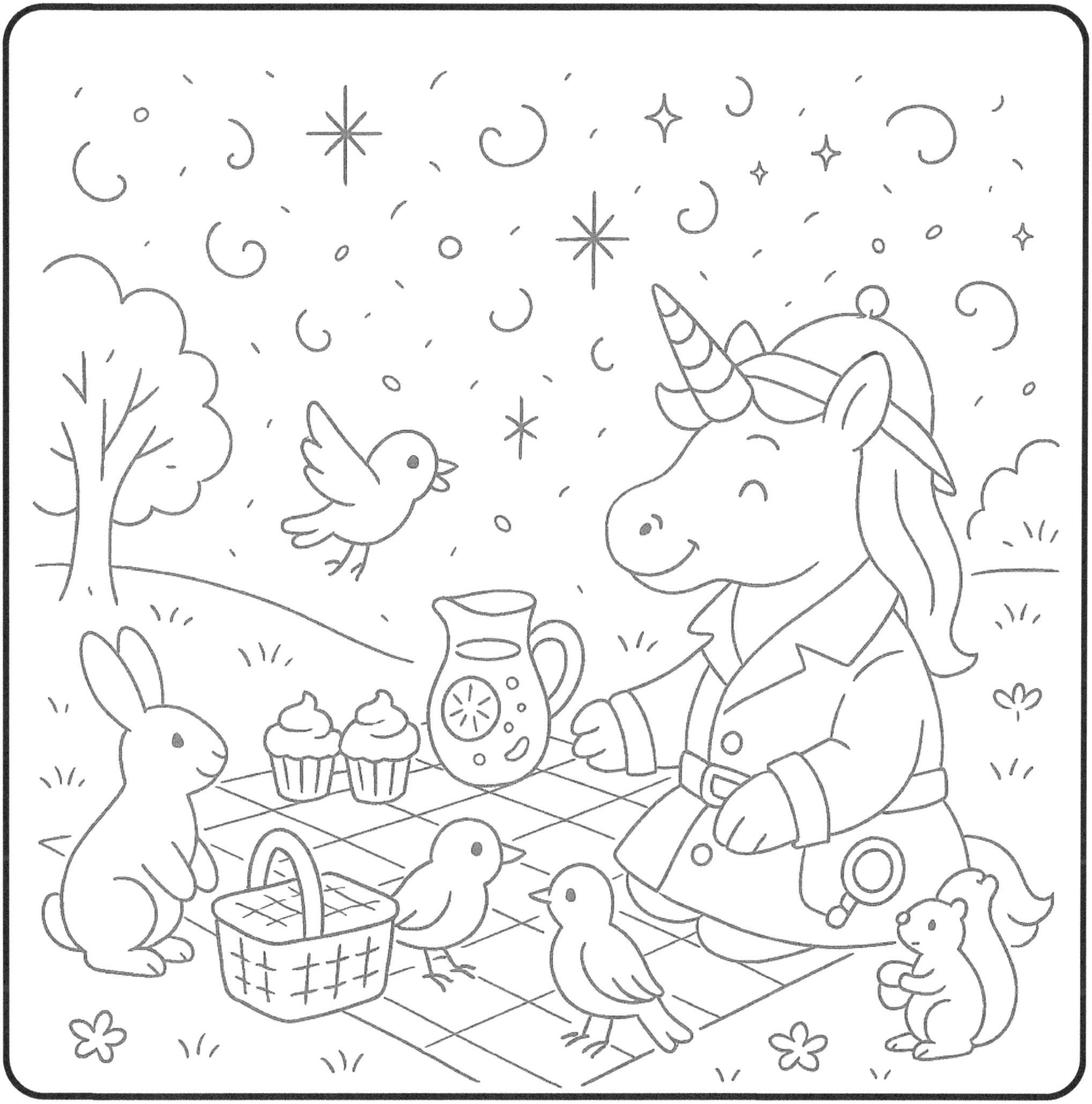

THE END

Thanks to Detective Sparklehoof's kindness, curiosity, and hard work, the town discovered their missing glitter hadn't been stolen – it had simply floated away with the river.

With a little teamwork, lots of laughter, and a sprinkle of hope, they brought the magic back brighter than ever.

Streamers danced, fireworks lit up the stars, and every creature big and small celebrated the joy of working together.

Thank You for Joining Detective Sparklehoof's Adventure!

You followed the clues, chased the sparkle, and helped bring magic back to the town.

Never stop being curious, kind, and brave—because the world is full of mysteries waiting for someone just like you to solve them.

Until the next adventure...

ABOUT

At Magic Pony Printables, we believe creativity should be fun, cozy, and a little bit magical. We create adorable coloring books, activity pages, and printable adventures designed to spark imagination and bring extra joy.

Follow along on Instagram: @magic_pony_printables

scan here

Made in the USA
Las Vegas, NV
07 May 2025